Little Owl's Snow

by Divya Srinivasan

VIKING

A chill cut through the forest.
Little Owl fluffed his feathers.

"Something is happening!" he thought.

Green leaves turned

orange,

gold,

and brown,

and then began to fall.

Geese flew off to warmer places,
navigating by starlight, and
honking all the way.

Dry, fallen leaves rustled and crackled,
as animals scurried, preparing for the cold.

Bear was eating all day, and into the night.
"Winter's almost here!" Little Owl said.
"Isn't it exciting?"
"Winter's too COLD!" Bear shuddered.
"I'm staying in."

"Bear sleeps through all the fun,"
Raccoon whispered. "You'll see."

Bats disappeared into a cave.
Caterpillars closed up their cocoons.

"Goodbye," Hedgehog called. "See you in spring!"
And he wiggled into his warm winter home.

Little Owl thought he saw a moth!

But it was only a leaf in the wind.
The forest felt so empty now.

HHHHHHAAAAAAA

The friends were making fog
when it happened . . .

. . . snow!

Soon, the forest was blanketed in snow, its crystals glinting in the light.

Tracks began to appear.
Not everyone was hidden away.

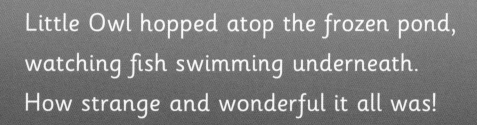

Little Owl hopped atop the frozen pond,
watching fish swimming underneath.
How strange and wonderful it all was!

But one night, Little Owl started
to miss Hedgehog.

"Mama," Little Owl asked,
"how much longer till spring?"

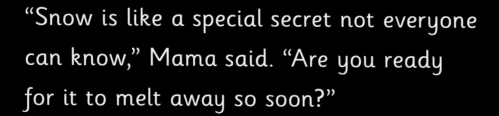

"Snow is like a special secret not everyone
can know," Mama said. "Are you ready
for it to melt away so soon?"

The forest was very quiet.
Little Owl could hear the smallest sounds.

Tap . . .   tap . . .
An icicle dripped onto a patch of slush.

Mama told Little Owl he would see
fireflies again. He would see
Hedgehog too, soon enough.

Right now, though . . . .

. . . . it was time to enjoy the snow.

Thank you to Uma, for wanting to hear it "again!"
And to Amma and Appa, for giving me time.
Love, Amma/Divya

VIKING

Penguin Young Readers
An imprint of Penguin Random House LLC
375 Hudson Street
New York, New York 10014

First published in the United States of America by Viking,
an imprint of Penguin Random House LLC, 2018

LIBRARY OF CONGRESS CATALOGING-IN-PUBLICATION DATA IS AVAILABLE.
ISBN 9780670016518

1 3 5 7 9 10 8 6 4 2

Manufactured in China   Set in Sassoon Infant